Visiting You

REBECKA SHARPE SHELBERG & ANDREA EDMONDS

We caught the train to visit
you today. There were so
many people, Mama held
my hand real tight.

We stood next to a man so tall
he could touch the roof without
stretching. He looked scruffy
and gruff but I wasn't scared.

'Who are you going to visit?' I asked him.

'My little girl,' he replied, and with a wide smile he told me about his daughter.

How they play dress up ...

how they swing so high ...

and how they read
together every evening
before he goes home.

'I miss her when I'm not with her,' he says, and
I can tell he loves her as much as I love you.

We took the bus to visit you today. 'Almost missed you!' the driver exclaimed.

We sat next to an old man with hair like white fairy floss and a big round nose. He looked gruff and grouchy but I wasn't scared.

'Who are you going to visit?'
I asked him.

'My old Millie,' he replied,
and with a wistful smile he
told me about his wife.

How one moment she'd scold him but kiss him the next ...
how they never ran out of laughter or things to say ...

and how she now stays on the hill next to the church where he visits her every day.

'I miss her all the time,' he says, and I can tell he loves her as much as I love you.

We caught the tram to visit you today.

A girl sat next to us with hair as black as the night and a ring through her nose. She looked grouchy and cross but I wasn't scared.

'Who are you going to visit?' I asked her. 'My Aja,' she said, and with a smile in her eyes she told me about her Grandad.

How he taught her to fish ...

swim and ride a bike ...

how he always called her 'Princess' even when she rolled her eyes, and how his memory had got so bad that he'd forgotten who she was.

'I really miss how he used to be,' she says, and I can tell she loves him as much as I love you.

We caught the ferry to visit you today.

We sat across from a woman as big as a bear, with tattoos down her arm. She looked cross and worried but I wasn't scared.

'Who are you going to visit?' I asked her.

'My silly Luke,' she replied, and with a grimace in her smile she told me about her son.

How he used to climb
giant trees and get stuck
all the way at the top ...

how he'd ride a roller
coaster with a straight
face while everyone
else was screaming ...

and how he'd fallen
off his motorcycle and
had been asleep in the
hospital ever since.

'I really miss his smile,' she says, and I can tell she loves him as much as I love you.

We drove our car to visit you today. There is just us and the radio. Mama looks worried and tired, but I'm not scared. I tell her that you'll be all right.

I tell her that you must miss us more than anything else in the world.

WELCOME
TO
HOPE MEADOWS

Mama gives me a wobbly
smile and I smile back.

I smile wide because
we have arrived.

And now it's time
for visiting you.

For Greg Hirst, enormously loved and dreadfully missed.
— R.S.S.

For my Mum and Dad, Yvonne and Gene.
Thank you for your love and encouragement.
— A.E.

First published 2018

EK Books
an imprint of Exisle Publishing Pty Ltd
PO Box 864, Chatswood, NSW 2057, Australia
226 High Street, Dunedin, 9016, New Zealand
www.ekbooks.org

A CiP record for this book is available from the National
Library of Australia.

ISBN 978-1-925335-66-8

Designed by Big Cat Design
Typeset in Minion Pro 17 on 25pt
Printed in China

This book uses paper sourced under ISO 14001 guidelines
from well-managed forests and other controlled sources.

10 9 8 7 6 5 4 3 2 1